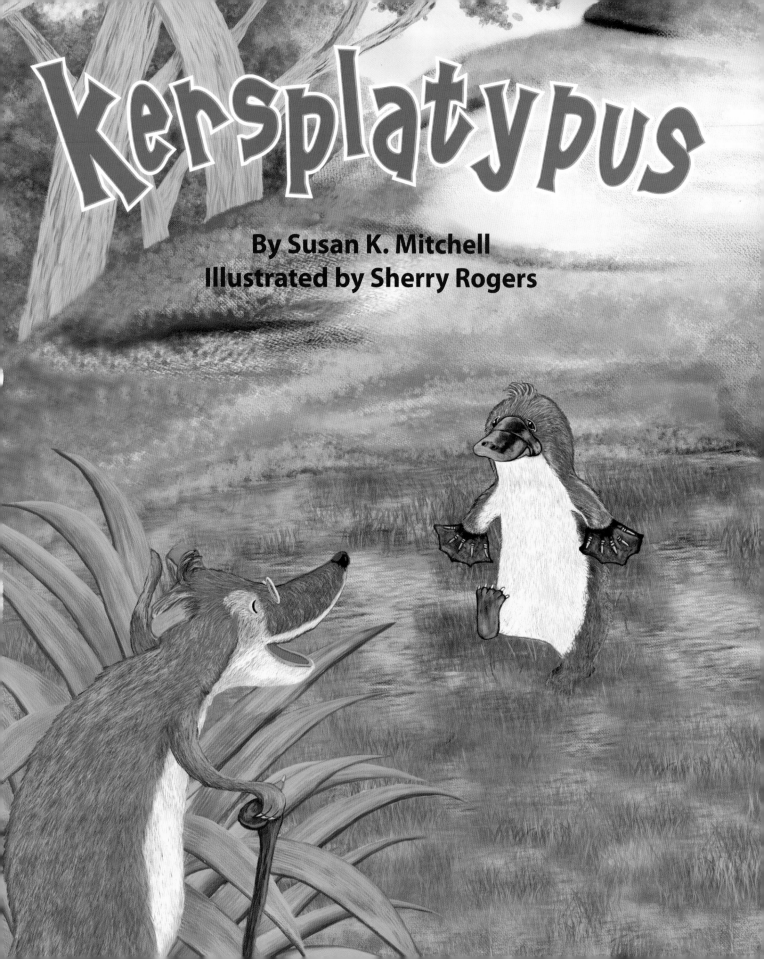

Kersplatypus

By Susan K. Mitchell

Illustrated by Sherry Rogers

The creature definitely did not belong there. Outback animals gathered around the tiny, damp thing in the grass.

"*Crikey*, what's that?" said Brushtail Possum.

"I've never seen anything like it," said Kookaburra.

"Must have been washed here by the big rains," said Wallaby.

The little creature had a flat, furry body. It had webbed feet and a scoopy duck bill.

"You're the craziest looking thing I've ever seen," said Blue-Tongued Skink. "What are you supposed to be?"

"I don't know," said the creature. "I don't know how I got here. The last place I remember was cozy, warm, and dark. The next thing I knew there was a big rumble and a wet tumble. Then I landed here. Do any of you know where I belong?"

The other animals stood and stared. They watched and wondered. Brushtail Possum looked at the fur on his body and the claws on the tips of the creature's toes. They were very much like her claws. "You must belong in a tree," she said, "follow me."

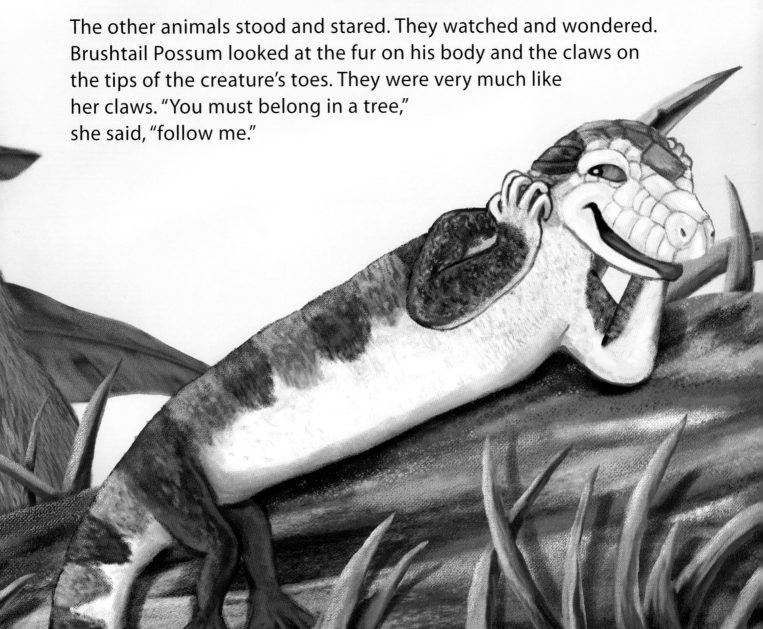

She led the creature to the forest. Brushtail Possum used her claws and scampered up a tree trunk. She sat on a branch and waited.

The little creature grabbed the trunk of the tree, started to climb and . . .

KERSPLAT! He fell flat.

"I don't think I belong in a tree," he said.

Blue-Tongued Skink simply laughed.

Kookaburra looked at the creature's webbed feet and scoopy duck bill. They were very much like other birds she had seen.

"You must belong in the air," she said, "follow me."

She led the creature to a large rock. Kookaburra raced across the rock, and when she got to the end, she flapped her wings and soared. She looked down and waited.

The little creature waddled as fast as he could to the end of the rock, flapped his webbed feet and . . .

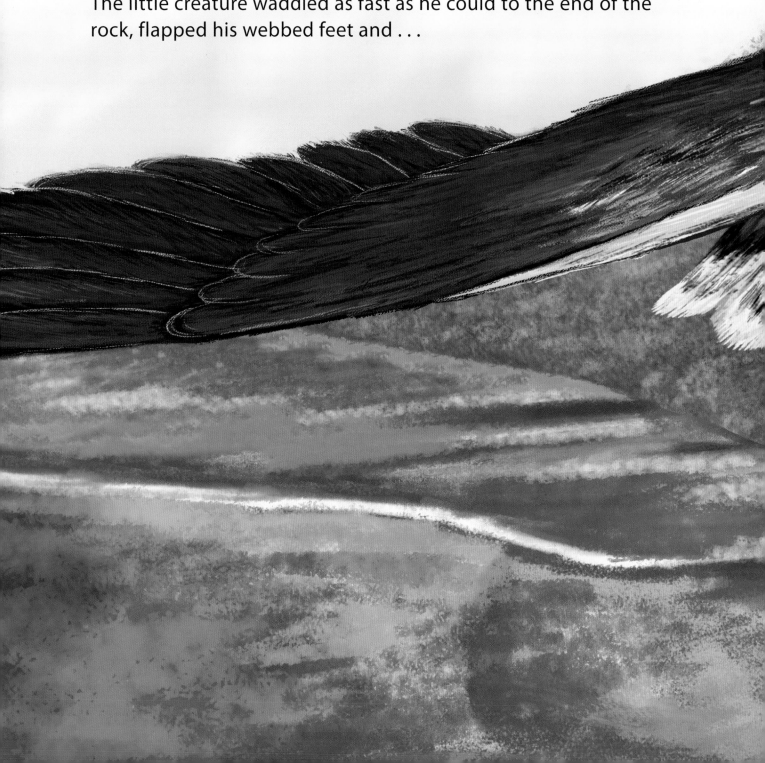

KERSPLAT! He fell flat.

"I don't think I belong in the air," he said.

Blue-Tongued Skink just laughed.

Wallaby looked at the creature's tail. It was not like her own, but a tail just the same.

"You must belong on the ground," she said, "follow me."

She led the creature to a clearing in the forest. Wallaby balanced on her tail and bounced high in the air. She bounded around in a circle. Then she sat back and waited.

The little creature flapped his flat tail, jumped up and . . .

KERSPLAT! He fell flat and began to cry.

"I don't think I belong on the ground either," he said. "Maybe I don't belong anywhere."

Blue-Tongued Skink simply laughed.

Just then, Old Bandicoot happened by. He was out digging for food and saw the commotion.

"*G'day mates!* What seems to be the problem here?" he asked.

Brushtail Possum wiped tears from the creature's tiny black eyes.

"This here fella doesn't know what he is," answered Kookaburra.

"Or where he belongs," said Wallaby.

"Hmmm, let me see," said Bandicoot. "I've heard of a creature like this: a furry body, webbed feet, and a scoopy duck bill. Pretty sure it's called a Platypus but sorry, I can't tell ya where he belongs."

Blue-Tongued Skink couldn't control his laughter. He held his belly and rolled around and around.

"Platypus?" he teased. "He can't climb. He can't fly. He can't hop. So far, all he's good at is falling flat. He's not a platypus . . . he's a KERSPLATYPUS!"

"Don't listen to him, mate," said Bandicoot, as he walked back into the brush. "You'll figure it out."

"At least now I have a name," said Platypus.

So Platypus set out on a walkabout, and his new friends followed.

"I wouldn't miss this for anything," cried Blue-Tongued Skink.

Platypus waddled to the edge of the forest and made his way past the billabongs to a river.

The water looked cool and inviting—not like the rumbling, tumbling big rains that had washed him away. He stuck a webbed foot in the water, and then before you could say "Waltzing Matilda," he jumped right in!

Platypus dipped and dove. He flipped and flopped and felt right at home.

Suddenly, Platypus saw something that seemed slightly familiar. It was a creature with a flat, furry body . . .

. . . just like him. It had webbed feet and a scoopy duck bill, and it was swimming his way!

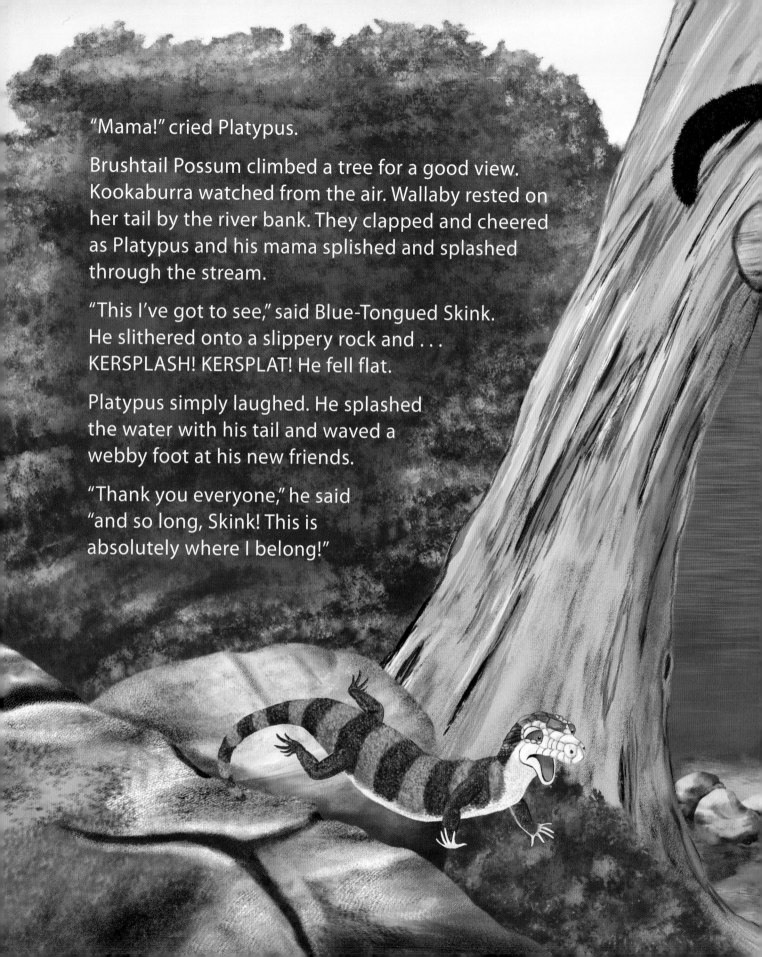

"Mama!" cried Platypus.

Brushtail Possum climbed a tree for a good view. Kookaburra watched from the air. Wallaby rested on her tail by the river bank. They clapped and cheered as Platypus and his mama splished and splashed through the stream.

"This I've got to see," said Blue-Tongued Skink. He slithered onto a slippery rock and . . . KERSPLASH! KERSPLAT! He fell flat.

Platypus simply laughed. He splashed the water with his tail and waved a webby foot at his new friends.

"Thank you everyone," he said "and so long, Skink! This is absolutely where I belong!"

For Creative Minds

Platypus Fun Facts

Wild platypuses are found in AUSTRALIA.

Their fur is very thick to keep them dry and warm, even in cold water.

They are mammals just like us, but they lay eggs (monotreme) instead of having live babies!

The babies lap up milk that oozes from pores on the mother's stomach.

Their tails are long and flat to help them steer through the water.

When they are about four months old, they swim for the first time. Until then, they stay in their underground burrow.

They live on the sides of rivers and lakes in burrows that are up to 50 feet long.

Because they spend so much time in the water, their front feet are webbed like a duck and the toes stretch into "paddles" for swimming. Their back feet are used to help steer and are only partly webbed.

They close their eyes and ears when they dive for food.

If necessary, they can stay underwater for up to 10 minutes to hide from predators.

Outback Animal Adaptation Activity

a. Platypus (fur)
The duck-like bill is both a nose and mouth. This long, funny-looking bill is packed with thousands of sensors. They help the platypus find food by sensing any movement made by prey (worms and other little animals).

_____ 1.

b. Brushtail Possum (fur)
These marsupials have prehensile tails that are used like hands to grab and hold onto things. They also have very sharp claws to hold onto tree branches. They eat leaves, flowers, fruits, and seeds.

_____ 2.

c. Kookaburra (feathers)
Kookaburras are known for their loud, "laughing" call at dawn and dusk. They have claws facing forward and backward to help hold onto tree branches. They eat worms, bugs, and other small animals.

_____ 3.

d. Wallaby (fur)
These marsupials use their tails to help balance. They also use their tails to steer when they jump forward. They eat a variety of plants.

_____ 4.

e. Blue-Tongued Skink (scaly skin)
When scared, they open their mouths wide, and their bright blue tongues scare off predators. They eat both plants and small animals.

_____ 5.

f. Bandicoot (fur)
These marsupials use their snouts to dig for food. They smell and hear very well but don't see very well. They eat both plants and small animals.

_____ 6.

Use the information above to determine which animals are carnivores (meat eaters), herbivores (plant eaters), or omnivores (both plants and animals)? What are you?

Answers: a.5, b.4, c.1, d.2, e.3, f.6

Animal Classification

When sorting, the first question scientists will ask is whether the item is (or was) alive. Both plants and animals are living things.

If the item in question is an animal, like the animals in the story, scientists will then ask other questions:

Does it have hair or fur, feathers, dry skin, or scales?
Does it breathe air through lungs or water through gills?
Are the babies born alive or hatched from eggs?
Does the baby drink milk from its mother?
Is it warm or cold-blooded?
How many body parts does the animal have?

By answering these (and other) questions, scientists can sort or classify the animals into "*classes*" such as *mammal, bird, reptile, fish, amphibian, or insect*.

Sometimes scientists have to make smaller groups within a bigger group to make everything "fit." For example, most mammal babies are born live instead of hatching from eggs. But, there are two mammals that hatch from eggs: the platypus and several types of echidnas.

Look on a map or globe to find the continent of Australia. Because it is so isolated, there are some animals that live only there. It is the only place in the world where you can find all three subclasses (smaller groups) of mammals:

Placental   babies are born alive and well-developed (humans, cats & dogs)
Marsupials   babies are born, then grow and develop inside the mother's pouch
Monotrems   babies are hatched from eggs

The animals in this book are from three different animal classes. Using information found in the book, can you then match the animal to its class and its subclass? The answers are upside down on the bottom of the page.

Blue-Tongued Skink

Bandicoot

Wallaby

Kookaburra

Brushtail Possum

Platypus

 Does the animal have hair or fur? If so, it is a *mammal*.
        Are the babies born, then grow and develop inside their mothers' pouches?
        Are these mammals hatched from eggs?
Does it have feathers? If so, it is a *bird.*
Does it have dry skin or scales? If so, it is a *reptile*.

mammals:

bird:
_____

marsupials:
_____
_____
_____

monotremes:
_____

reptile:
_____

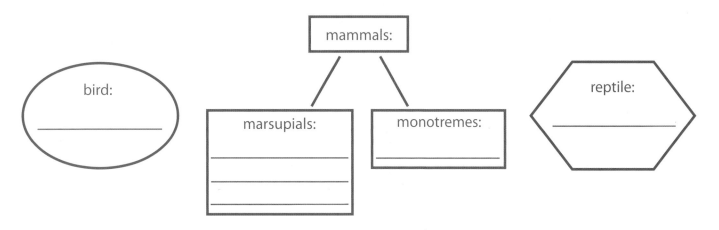

Bully or Friend?

What are some words to describe how you think the baby platypus might have felt when he was washed out of his burrow?

Who were the animals that were most helpful to the baby platypus?

Who was a bully that teased or made fun of the baby platypus?

Which animals would you like to have as friends? Why?

Which animals would you like to be most similar to and why?

Has anyone ever made fun of you? Did you like it? What did you do?

Who do you think you could talk to who would be able to help you?

For Emily, Rachel, and Joseph; with love and laughter always—SKM
To my husband Dale, and my children Josh and Rachel, who bring true joy to my life—SR

Thanks to Geoff Williams of the Australian Platypus Conservancy and to Ron Fricke, Deputy Director of the Toledo Zoo for verifying the accuracy of the information in this book

Publisher's Cataloging-In-Publication Data
Mitchell, Susan K.
Kersplatypus / by Susan K. Mitchell ; illustrated by Sherry Rogers.

p. : col. ill. ; cm.

Summary: When a strange little creature appears out of nowhere after the big rains,
Australian animals wonder what in the world he could possibly be!
With a "down-under" spirit, they all pitch in to help him discover where he belongs.
Includes "For Creative Minds" section with platypus fun facts and other activities.
Interest age level: 003-007.
Interest grade level: P-2.
ISBN: 978-1-934359-07-5 (hardcover)
ISBN: 978-1-934359-23-5 (pbk.)

1. Platypus--Juvenile fiction. 2. Friends--Juvenile fiction. 3. Teasing--Juvenile fiction.
4. Platypus--Fiction. 5. Friends--Fiction. 6. Teasing--Fiction. I. Rogers, Sherry II. Title.

PZ10.3.M58 Ke 2008[E]   2007935082

Printed in China

Sylvan Dell Publishing
976 Houston Northcutt Blvd., Suite 3
Mt. Pleasant, SC 29464